My Dad
The
Dragon
by Jackie French

illustrated by Stephen Michael King

Librarian Reviewer
Marci Peschke
Librarian, Dallas Independent School District
MA Education Reading Specialist, Stephen F. Austin State University
Learning Resources Endorsement, Texas Women's University

Reading Consultant
Sherry Klehr
Elementary/Middle School Educator, Edina Public Schools, MN
MA in Education, University of Minnesota

STONE ARCH BOOKS
Minneapolis   San Diego

First published in the United States in 2007
by Stone Arch Books,
151 Good Counsel Drive, P.O. Box 669,
Mankato, Minnesota 56002
www.stonearchbooks.com

First published in English in Sydney, Australia,
by HarperCollins Publishers Australia Pty Ltd in 2004.
This English language edition is published by arrangement
with HarperCollins Publishers Australia Pty Ltd.

Library of Congress Cataloging-in-Publication Data
French, Jackie.
    My Dad the Dragon / by Jackie French ; illustrated by Stephen
Michael King.
        p. cm. — (Funny Families)
    "Pathway Books."
    Summary: Horace has received an almost impossible homework
assignment at King Arthur's School for Trainee Knights—he has to kill a
dragon, which is even more difficult because his father is one.
    ISBN-13: 978-1-59889-343-4 (library binding)
    ISBN-10: 1-59889-343-2 (library binding)
    ISBN-13: 978-1-59889-436-3 (paperback)
    ISBN-10: 1-59889-436-6 (paperback)
    [1. Dragons—Fiction. 2. Knights and knighthood—Fiction.
3. Schools—Fiction. 4. Middle Ages—Fiction.] I. King, Stephen Michael,
ill. II. Title.
PZ7.F88903Mx 2007
[Fic]—dc22   2006027144

1 2 3 4 5 6 12 11 10 09 08 07

Printed in the United States of America

Table of Contents

Table of Contents
Continued

CHAPTER 1

Horrible Homework

"Now for your homework!" announced Sir Sneazle, smiling nastily at the class. Sir Sneazle's teeth were sharp and yellow, and he showed too many of them when he smiled.

Sir Sneazle's eyes were black and cold. "This weekend's homework is important," he said. "His Majesty, King Arthur, is going to inspect the school on Monday morning. He will want to see your homework!"

Horace groaned. Sir Sneazle never smiled at anything good.

"Now," said Sir Sneazle, "Bernard, your homework will be a hundred-page report on the history of the sword."

"A hundred pages, sir?" whispered Bernard. He was the best sword fighter in the whole school, even better than some of the Knights of the Round Table. But whenever Bernard tried to use a feather pen, the ink smudged all over the page.

"A hundred pages," Sir Sneazle said. "And no blots! If there is a single blot, I will tear the whole thing up! Bran, Pol, and Snidge, your homework is to rescue a maiden in distress." He smiled again.

"Make sure she's here first thing Monday morning, and make sure she's a real maiden. This maiden has to be young and beautiful."

Bran, Pol, and Snidge looked horrified. "But, sir," said Pol.

"Silence," roared Sir Sneazle. Sir Sneazle's roar was almost as bad as his evil smile.

"Now, Horace," Sir Sneazle said. "What can little Horace do? I know! I have the perfect little project to keep you busy."

"Yes, sir?" asked Horace.

"You can bring us a dragon," said Sir Sneazle. "A dead dragon."

"But no one kills dragons anymore, sir!" cried Horace. "They're a protected species! And we've never been taught how to kill a dragon, sir."

Sir Sneazle stared at him. "Any boy who doesn't do his homework will be expelled! A note will be made on his record so he can never ever be made a Knight of the Round Table! Or any other table! You understand?"

"Yes, sir," whispered Horace.

"Now, class dismissed!"

CHAPTER 2

Kill a Dragon?

Sir Sneazle swept out of the classroom.
A cold breeze seemed to follow him.
Horace sat, stunned.

A dragon! How could he possibly tell
Mom and Dad he had to catch and kill
a dragon?

"A hundred pages," whispered
Bernard. "I can't write a hundred pages! I
can't write half a page without blots!"

"A maiden!" Snidge's red ears were
even redder.

"I tried asking a maiden to dance once and she laughed!" Pol was nearly in tears.

"I can't help it if I smell!" said Bran. "You can't work with pigs and not stink! What maiden is going to even look at the three of us, much less let us rescue her?!"

"We can fix this!" Horace said. "How about you all come over tomorrow? We can all help Bernard write his report."

Bernard nodded. "I know everything about swords. I'm just no good with feather pens."

Horace nodded. "Then we'll find a maiden to rescue."

"We're just kids!" said Snidge. "No maiden will take us seriously!"

"We can ask my mom to turn us into knights for a day," Horace said. Mom's spells didn't always work. But turning five boys into knights for an afternoon couldn't be too hard, even for Mom! "Then all we have to do is find a maiden, rescue her, and ask her to come to school on Monday morning," he added.

"But we won't be handsome knights on Monday!" said Snidge.

"Who cares?" said Horace. "She just has to come to school!"

Bernard grinned. "Then all of us can help you find your dragon!"

"My uncle Slodge says he saw a dragon last week!" cried Snidge.

"I'm sure a dragon has been stealing our pigs!" said Bran.

Horace gulped. "No," he said. "Thanks anyway. I think I'd better find a dragon all by myself."

CHAPTER 3

Mom Tries to Help

It was a long walk home, but Horace enjoyed it. The fields shone gold in the autumn sunlight.

It hadn't always been so peaceful. Before Horace was born, the country was in a war. The Saxons had invaded, trying to claim the land as their own.

Then King Arthur had pulled the magic sword from the stone and called all the great knights to be with him. The Saxons had to leave the country.

One day, thought Horace, he'd be a knight too. His name would be written on his chair at the Round Table and he would protect the land from evil and make his family proud.

Home looked peaceful. The little rose-covered cottage nestled against the hillside. The cottage looked tiny, but it was larger than it looked. There were caves in the hill connected to the cottage. Dad had turned one into his study, and Mom and Dad's bedroom was in another.

Horace walked up the crooked path between the flowers and the guinea pig bushes.

Mom had been trying to
conjure up rose bushes, but
the baby guinea pigs on the
bushes looked cute anyway.
They wrinkled up their little
noses as their bushes blew in
the wind. When the guinea
pigs grew older, they dropped
off the stems and ran around. Guinea
pigs were more interesting than roses,
thought Horace, even if Mom said they
didn't smell as good.

Mom was already cooking dinner
when Horace entered the kitchen.

"Eye of spider, tongue of bat," she
muttered, throwing something brown
and wrinkled into the cauldron. "Hello,
Horace darling! Stir it up and that is that.
I hope anyway," she murmured, peering
into the cauldron.

Bunnnggg! The cauldron exploded. Suddenly dinner was on the table. The kitchen was quiet.

"Mom," said Horace, staring at the dinner.

"Yes?" said Mom.

"What is it?"

"It should be roast lamb," said Mom. "That's what the spell said, anyway."

"I don't think lamb has tentacles," Horace pointed out.

"Are you sure?" Mom poked the roast, then stepped back as the dinner snarled.

"I don't think roast lamb is supposed to be purple, either," added Horace.

"Maybe I overdid the garlic," admitted Mom. "Or not enough slug vomit."

"Isn't there something else you could use instead of slug vomit?" asked Horace, trying not to sound ungrateful.

"I'm all out of unicorn horn," explained Mom. "Anyway, I'm sure it'll taste like lamb," she added. "It'll probably stop wiggling soon. How was school?"

Horace sighed. Mom and Dad were so proud he'd been accepted into the King's school. How could he tell them how bad things were?

"It was okay," he said. "Mom, do you think you could turn us all into handsome knights? It's for our homework project."

"Knights, knights." Mom looked through her spell book. "Knapsack, knife, hmmm. Are you sure you wouldn't like to be knapsacks?"

"No, Mom. We have to be knights. Handsome knights," repeated Horace.

"Not knapsacks. Okay," said Mom. She smiled at Horace. "Could you go tell Dad and Grub that dinner's ready? Lie down, you stupid roast! Shoo! Get back on that table!"

"Maybe we could just have scrambled eggs," said Horace. Dinner tried to jump out the kitchen window. He picked up his school bag and wandered down the hall.

CHAPTER 4

Grub the Inventor

Grub was in her bedroom.

"Hi," Horace said. "Dinner's ready."

Grub looked up from her latest invention. It had two giant wheels and a funny seat on top. Grub's overalls were even grubbier than they had been yesterday, and her braids looked like she'd used them to mop up an oil stain.

Grub's real name was Fair Elayne, but Horace thought Grub was better. "Is dinner really ready?" Grub asked.

"It was trying to jump out the kitchen window," said Horace. "But you'd better wash your hands anyway." He stared at Grub's invention. "What's that thing?"

"Like it?" Grub stood back. "I invented it this morning!"

"What does it do?" asked Horace.

"You sit on it and push the pedals with your feet to make the wheels go around, and it takes you wherever you point it," Grub explained.

"Hmm," said Horace. "It'll never catch on. Who wants to push pedals when you can sit on a horse?"

Grub sighed. "Maybe you're right. How was school? I wish I could go to school," she added.

"Girls don't go to school," pointed out Horace. "They can't become knights, so why go to school?" He shrugged. "It was okay."

Grub looked at him. "Are you sure?"

Horace gulped. How could he tell any member of his family that he had to hunt — and kill — a dragon?

"I'd better go tell Dad it's dinnertime," he said. "You'd better wash the grease off your face, too!"

Grub poked her tongue out at him.

Horace shoved his school bag into his bedroom, then hurried down the hall to the door to the caves below the mountain.

It was just a plain wooden door, with a big sign saying, "Keep Out! This means you kids. I mean it! Love, Dad."

Horace knocked on the door, then knocked again when there was no answer. "Hey, Dad," he yelled. "It's dinnertime."

Keep Out!
This means you kids.
I mean it!
Love, Dad.

"Coming!" yelled Dad.

Horace trotted down the hall to set the table.

CHAPTER 5

Dad the Dragon

Dinner was scrambled eggs on toast. There was no sign of the roast lamb, except for some purple footprints across the floor.

Mom sat at one end of the table, with Horace and Grub on either side. Horace reached for a slice of toast just as Dad came in.

Whump! The doorway crashed around his tail.

Whump!

Crack! The chair splintered as he sat down.

Dad's tail knocked a plant over.

Mom sighed. "Dear, I wish you'd remember to change for dinner."

"Oops." Dad stared down at his glittering scales, his silver wings, and his green and orange tail that reached into the hallway. Bunngg! Dad returned to human form. He pulled up another chair and sat down. "Sorry about that, everyone."

Sometimes Horace wished Dad would decide to be something else besides a dragon for a change.

Something smaller, like a gorilla, or even an eagle. But Dad liked being a dragon! Luckily it seemed to be the one spell of Mom's that always worked.

Horace shook his head. How could he tell Dad that he had to hunt and kill a dragon and bring it to school on Monday? Dad would never understand.

"How was school?" asked Dad, chewing a spoonful of scrambled eggs.

"Oh, fine," said Horace, crossing his fingers under the table. "Some of the boys are coming over tomorrow so we can do our homework together."

Dad nodded. "I'll remember to stay human after breakfast," he promised. He stared at Grub. "What is that you're using on your scrambled eggs?"

Horace peered at the object as Grub handed it over the table.

It looked like a spoon, but it had three points.

"It's sort of like a pitchfork, only smaller," said Grub. "I invented it this afternoon. I thought it would be easier to pick up food with instead of just a knife and spoon."

Dad snorted, sending toast crumbs flying. "A hay fork!" boomed Dad. "No daughter of mine eats with a hay fork!"

"But, Dad," began Grub.

"No bad manners at this table, young lady! You'll eat with a spoon and your fingers, and wipe your chin neatly on the tablecloth like the rest of us!" Dad stopped. "Ooops! Horace, grab the water jug," he added. "I seem to have set the curtains on fire with my breath. Now, what's for dessert?"

CHAPTER 6

Is That a Real Dragon?

Horace lay in bed and worried. Outside the window an owl hooted. Dad's snores echoed from the cave.

Dad would never understand his son wanting to kill a dragon! There has to be some way out of this, thought Horace.

Maybe he could make a model of a dragon. But no, Sir Sneazle would notice it wasn't real!

Maybe Mom could cast a spell! But Mom's spells didn't always work.

No, there was no way out of it, Horace decided. He'd have to find a dragon, fight it, and bring its body to school! He just had to become a knight!

Suddenly something tiptoed down the hall. Something large, with a tail that dragged behind.

Horace grinned. It was Dad, sneaking down to the kitchen for a snack. He often got hungry in the middle of the night.

Things would work out, Horace decided. He snuggled into his bed.

Grark! Grark! Grark!

Horace sprang up from his pillow. What was that? A fox after the hens? No hen screamed like that! It seemed to come from up in the sky!

Horace's heart pounded. He raced down the hall and out the front door.

There in the sky was
a dragon. Its giant
scales gleamed in
the moonlight. Its
wings looked like
golden clouds. Its tail
flickered across the sky.

Something large and pink wiggled in its
mouth, then it screamed again.

Oooiiiinnnkkkkkkk!

The dragon glided lower and lower.
Horace let out his breath in disappointment.
"It's Dad," he sighed.

Dad landed in the gooseberry bed. He
hopped out of the gooseberry bushes and
rose on his back legs to pull the thorns
out of his wings.

"Dad!" cried Horace. "What are
you doing?"

Dad jumped. "Just having a snack," he muttered with a the pig in his mouth.

"Is that one of Bran's pigs?" demanded Horace. "Dad, how could you?"

Dad spit the pig out. It squealed and ran under the guinea pig bushes, where it peered out cautiously.

"Oink!" it muttered.

Dad hung his head. "A plate of scrambled eggs isn't enough for a dragon for dinner," he said.

"But, Dad, you can't steal pigs! Take it back and I'll make you some toast!"

Dad smiled. "Toast with blackberry jam?"

"With blackberry jam," agreed Horace.

"Then I'll take the pig back," said Dad. "Here piggie, piggie."

"Dad, I think you're scaring the pig," said Horace.

"What? Oh."

Bunnnggg! Suddenly Dad was human again. The pig peered out at him, then trotted out onto the path.

Dad sighed. "Life is much simpler as a dragon. Come on, pig. I'll be back in an hour or two," he added to Horace.

"I'll have the toast ready," promised Horace. Dad and the pig headed off into the moonlight.

"Oink," said the pig.

CHAPTER 7

A Spell Goes Wrong

"Kelpie, kidney," said Mom, flipping though her spell book. "Knack, knife. Ah, knight, here we are. Knight on horseback, knight in armor, knight, very handsome."

"That's the one," said Horace.

Bran gazed at Mom. "Are you sure this is going to work?" he asked.

"Of course," said Mom. "I need three hairs from a dog's tail. Pass me the jar of dog's hair, Horace. A pinch of cockroach and three shakes of an earthworm's tail."

"My great-great-great-aunt Globb was enchanted once," said Snidge. "No one could wake her up for a hundred years."

"Did a handsome prince kiss her and wake her up?" asked Bran, interested.

"Nah. She woke up by herself. Was she ever hungry! Her teeth were all yellow and rotten. Mice had nested in her hair, too," said Snidge.

"Yuck," said Bernard. "If I was a handsome prince I wouldn't kiss a woman who was a hundred years old and had mice in her hair."

"If you were a handsome prince, we wouldn't be in this mess!" said Horace. "What else do you need, Mom?"

"Just my glasses," said Mom, looking at the tiny writing on the page. "I can't read this word. Thanks, pet," she added as Horace passed the glasses to her. "Cat? Rat? Bat?"

"I think it's lizard's fat," said Bran, staring over her shoulder.

"No, it's not. It's hat," said Mom. "I think it means I have to wear my hat for this. Okay, here we go."

"Black dog's hair and earthworm's tail, cockroach dung will never fail. In the cauldron, left to right, when it boils they're handsome . . ."

"Slugs!" called Horace from under the chair. "Mom, you turned us into slugs! No, we're down here! Look out, Mom. You almost stepped on Bran!"

"Oh dear," said Mom. "Maybe that word was bat! Or mat. Now if I just add a bit of doormat. Cauldron, cauldron, do not bite, when I wave my wand they're handsome . . ."

Five handsome elephants waved their trunks at her.

"Mom!" hooted Horace, trying not to crush the kitchen table.

"I know, I know," said Mom sadly. "Just let me try again."

"Darling cauldron, what a sight, five brave and handsome . . ."

"Oh, dear," said Mom.

A cockroach waved its feeler at her.

The cockroach sighed. "Mom, don't you think you should practice the handsome knight spell on something else first? Like the hens maybe."

"Good idea, Horace," Mom said.

"Mom!"

"Yes, darling?"

"Turn us back into kids again before you go."

CHAPTER 8

Grub's Little Invention

"So much for that idea," said Bran.

"I'm sorry," said Horace.

Snidge shook his head. "It's not your fault. You tried. Your Mom tried, too." He sighed. "I guess there's no spell in the world powerful enough to make us handsome!"

"I'm sure Mom will work the spell out some time," said Horace, glancing out the window, where Mom was practicing the spell.

Now three good-looking goats, a pretty pink monkey, and a very handsome banana with legs clucked around the hen yard. "How about we do the hundred-page report instead?" Horace said.

Horace opened a drawer and pulled out five feather pens, a bottle of ink, and a sheet of blotting paper. Bernard took one hundred sheets of manuscript paper from his bag.

"Okay," said Horace. "Snidge, you start. Bran, you write a part about how swords are made, and I'll do the last hundred years. Pol, you do how to take care of your sword, and Bernard, you write about famous battles. That's just twenty pages each!"

"The History of the Sword," began Snidge. Five heads bent over the table as they got to work.

Silence filled the kitchen, broken only
by the scratch of pens on paper.

"Oh no," muttered Snidge. "I blotted
a page."

"So did I," admitted Pol.

Bernard looked up in dismay. "But Sir
Sneazle said no blots!" Snidge looked down
at the page helplessly. "It's impossible to
write a hundred pages without a single blot!
Even the King's own writers couldn't do it!"

"Everyone makes blots!" said Pol. "It's
what feather pens do! They blot!"

"No report," wailed Bernard, "and no maiden."

No dragon, either, thought Horace. We're doomed.

"What are you doing?" Horace looked around as Grub wandered into the kitchen. She had a stain on her overalls, and her braids were tied up in a greasy rag around her head.

"Homework," Horace muttered. "It's boy stuff. You wouldn't understand."

Grub looked at him. "What wouldn't I understand? I can do anything you can do!"

"Can you write a hundred pages on the history of the sword?" demanded Horace.

"No," Grub said. "I don't know anything about swords."

Snidge sniffed. "Well, we can't write a hundred pages either."

"We can write it," corrected Bernard. "We just keep leaving blots."

"Blots?" Grub looked at the messy pages on the kitchen table. "I can fix those."

"No," said Horace. "This is no time for your silly inventions."

"Silly? It would serve you right if I just let you blot away all day," said Grub. "But I won't, because I'm a kind, generous sister. You stay here and I'll be right back."

Snidge stared after her. "What's she going to do?"

"Probably get one of her dumb inventions," said Horace.

Grub ran back into the room. "Look," she said, holding up five long, thin objects. "Just what you need!"

The boys stared. "What are they?" asked Pol.

"No-drip pens!" cried Grub.

"What are no-drip pens?"

"They're like feather pens, but they don't drip all over the page, you drip. You can write fast with them," she added, handing them one each.

Horace took his slowly, in case it exploded. He dipped it into the inkwell, then watched as the ink ran off in a stream onto the table.

"Yuck," he said, wiping the ink quickly and hoping it wouldn't leave a bad stain. "These things don't work at all!"

"Not like that!" said Grub. She grabbed the pen from him and began to write. "See? You don't have to dip these pens in the inkwell! You just write!"

"Hey, this works!" cried Snidge.

"It's really great!" said Pol. "No blots!"

"Even I can write with one of these," yelled Bernard. "It makes writing easy! Hey, look at me, everyone. I'm writing!"

Horace turned to Grub. "You don't have an invention to make us handsome, do you?"

"I might," said Grub.

"What?" cried Snidge.

"Really?" cried Bran.

"Yes, it's in the shed," said Grub. "You'll have to look at it there."

CHAPTER 9

It's a What?

The boys stared at Grub's invention.

"What is it?" asked Bran.

"It's a bath," said Grub. "You fill it with hot water and you get into it."

"Get into it!" cried Pol in horror. "You'd cook!"

"Not that hot," said Grub. "Then you take this stuff." She held out a yellow block for them to see. "It's soap. You rub the soap onto your skin, and then you wash it off."

"That gets rid of pig smell?"
asked Bran.

"Yes," said Grub.

"And pimples?" asked Pol.

"I promise your pimples will have almost
vanished by tomorrow," said Grub.

The boys stared at the bath and soap.

"Maybe I should try it first," offered
Horace. After all, Grub was his sister.

"I'm sure it works!" said Snidge, glancing up at Grub. "Let's go and get the bucket of hot water. "

Grub grinned. "There's just one other thing," she warned.

"What?" asked Horace.

"You have to take your clothes off before you get into it," Grub said.

The boys looked horrified. Grub grinned. "That's why it's in the shed! Yell when you're finished."

CHAPTER 10
A Maiden Is Rescued

Bran sniffed his armpit. "I smell strange," he said.

"I don't smell at all!" said Pol.

"That's what's so strange," said Bran. "I've never not stunk before."

Snidge looked down. "My knees still stick out," he said, "and my ears."

Grub poked her head around the door. "I told you it would work," she said.

"Do you use this thing?" asked Horace.

"Every day," said Grub.

"No wonder you smell so nice," said Snidge. Then he blushed.

Grub looked at him. "Well, does that take care of your homework? You've got pens that don't blot and now you don't smell."

"We still have to rescue a maiden," said Horace.

"Do you know any maidens?" asked Pol.

Grub sighed. "Boys!" she said. "Sometimes you don't look past your own noses. Wait here." She left the shed.

"What's she going to get now?" asked Bernard.

"Your sister is cool," added Bran.

"Yeah," whispered Snidge.

"It's probably just another invention," said Horace. "Maybe she invented a mechanical maiden, you know, like a doll that talks and walks."

"Sir Sneazle would know it wasn't a real maiden," said Bran.

Snidge stared out the window. "Look! It's a maiden! A really beautiful maiden!"

Horace looked out the window. A maiden was walking down the path between the guinea pig bushes.

She wore a green silk dress and a tall hat with a veil that floated in the breeze. Her golden hair flowed down her back and her tiny slippers went pat, pat, pat on the gravel.

"It's a real maiden!" muttered Bran.

"She's so beautiful!" cried Snidge.

"No!" yelled Horace. "It's Grub!"

"She doesn't look like a Grub now," said Pol.

"Well, her real name's Fair Elayne," said Horace, as Fair Elayne floated through the shed door.

"Well?" she asked.

Horace let out a breath. It really was Grub! "You look different," he muttered.

"I changed my clothes and brushed my hair," said Fair Elayne, and suddenly she sounded just like Grub again. "That's all a maiden is," she added. "A girl with fancy clothes on. Well, how do I look?"

"Wonderful!" whispered Snidge.

Grub looked at him. "Well, all you have to do now is rescue me," she pointed out.

"What from?" asked Bran.

Grub sighed. "Do I have to do everything around here? Oh dear! Look!"

"What?" Five heads turned around.

"Help, help!" said Grub. "There's a guinea pig out there! A terrible, ferocious guinea pig!"

Horace blinked.
"But they can't save
you from a guinea pig!"

"Why not?" demanded Grub. "Help,
help," she added. "The horrible guinea
pig is about to attack!"

"Sir Sneazle didn't say what we had to
rescue her from," Snidge pointed out. "He
just said we had to rescue her!"

"Well, hurry up," said Grub. "It's
almost lunchtime!"

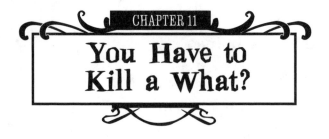

CHAPTER 11

You Have to Kill a What?

Lunch was hamburgers. Horace glanced at Dad. Thank goodness he remembered to change before he came out of the cave and into the cottage.

He looked normal sitting at the head of the table and joking with Bernard, Snidge, Bran, and Pol.

After apple pie and ice cream, Dad stood up from the table with a gentle burp. An apple pie burp, thought Horace, without any flash of dragon flame.

Horace heard Dad's feet go down the hall, then the sound that meant he opened the door to the cave under the hill, then shut it again.

What did Dad do all day under the hill? Horace wondered. Snidge's dad made swords and gates and cooking pots. Bran's dad looked after their pigs, Pol's dad made barrels, and Bernard's dad grew grains.

Horace's dad just disappeared back into his cave. Horace sighed. He had more important things to worry about now.

"Well," said Grub. "Have you got all your homework done yet?"

"One hundred-page report," said Snidge. "One maiden rescued. That only leaves one more thing."

"Nothing much," said Horace.

Pol stared at him. "Nothing much? You have to kill a . . ."

"Nothing!" interrupted Horace. "Really!"

Grub stared at him. "Exactly what do you have to kill, big brother?"

Horace sighed. There was no getting away from it now. "A dragon," he said.

Grub stared at him. "Your teacher wants you to kill a dragon?"

Horace nodded. "We are training to be knights. And knights kill dragons, or they used to, anyway."

"But you're still a kid!" Grub said, sounding shocked.

"I've noticed," said Horace.

Grub sat thinking for a minute. Horace waited for her to say something. Finally, all she said was, "Well."

"Well?" repeated Horace.

Grub nodded. "There's no way out. We just have to find you a dragon."

"It's my homework!" said Horace.

Snidge shook his head. "You helped us with our homework. We have to help you with yours."

"I found the solution to the other stuff, so if you have any brains, you'll let me help you," added Grub.

Horace bit his lip. "Dragon hunting can kill you," he said.

"Exactly!" said Grub. "That's why we're not going to let you do it by yourself!"

CHAPTER 12

Dragon Hunting

They climbed the hill above the cottage in silence. Finally Snidge pointed. "See that mountain," he said. "My dad says he's seen a dragon flying over there. It comes out of a cave in the cliffs."

"What does it look like?" asked Horace. Maybe it was Dad, not a real dragon.

"It was red, with great big wings."

Horace sighed in relief. Dad had gold scales! This had to be a real dragon after all! "Where is the cave?" Horace asked.

Grub handed him a small black thing with two circles pointing out. "Here, try this, big brother."

Horace looked at it. "What do you do with it?"

"If you look through the two circles, they make things look closer. I invented it last year."

"Really?" Horace said. "It might be useful!"

"All my inventions are useful," Grub said. "People just haven't caught up with them yet. Go on, try it."

Horace put the invention against his eyes.

"Wow!" he said. "The mountain looks like it's right here! I can see the cave, too! It's a great big black one!"

"I told you my inventions were useful," said Grub.

"Okay," said Snidge. "Let's get organized. We'll all meet at Horace and Grub's place tomorrow morning. I can borrow a sword for each of us! The wooden swords we use at school won't work against a dragon."

"I'll bring my dad's shield," offered Bernard.

"I'll bring the nets we use for catching pigs," said Bran. "Hey! I'll stand above the cave, and when the dragon comes out, I'll throw a net over it to trap it!"

"The rest of us will rush it, and Horace can kill it," said Snidge. "I wish we didn't have to kill the dragon," he added.

Bernard gulped. "I wish we didn't have to kill it either," he whispered. "But we do! Otherwise Horace will be kicked out of school."

And Mom and Dad will be ashamed forever, thought Horace.

"All right!" Horace said. "How about we meet at lunch instead, so we all get a good night's sleep?"

Grub looked at him. "Are you planning something, big brother?"

"Me? Of course not," said Horace. He crossed his fingers behind his back.

CHAPTER 13
Horace Goes Out Alone

Horace woke up early the next morning. It was almost dawn.

He dressed quickly. Dad's snores echoed down the hall as Horace crept out to the kitchen. For a moment he was tempted to wake up his parents. Maybe Mom could make him powerful, or Dad could help in the battle.

Horace shook his head. Dad loved dragons too much to ever fight one. The last time Mom had tried to make him powerful, she had given him a powerful smell instead.

It was still dark in the kitchen. Horace moved quietly through the room, grabbing a crust of bread and a hunk of cheese.

He gazed around the kitchen and then picked up a garbage can lid, a carving knife, and a broom.

The lid would have to be his shield, and if he tied the carving knife onto the broom handle, he could use it for a sword.

They weren't as good as a real sword and shield, but they were all he had.

Horace shook his head. How could he risk the lives of his friends to help him fight the dragon? It was his homework, not theirs.

Horace opened the front door and slipped outside. He grabbed the lid and broom, and trotted down the path.

The light grew stronger as he walked. He was glad now he'd brought the bread and cheese. He nibbled the food as he walked, then stopped to drink at a small stream. The water was cold and tasted icy.

The dragon mountain was growing closer. Horace could see the cave now. He could even smell dragon.

Horace gulped. It smelled like Dad, a hint of fire and hot rock. There was heat in the cold air too, as though something that breathed fire lived inside.

Maybe this dragon wouldn't look like Dad, thought Horace. Maybe this dragon was a wild monster and deserved to die!

Horace began to shiver. Did he really want to face a dragon?

It was either kill a dragon or be expelled! He stomped closer to the cave and took a deep breath for the dragon challenge. "Avaunt, dragon!" he squeaked. "Avaunt" was what knights said when they wanted to fight an enemy.

Horace waited. Maybe there wasn't a dragon here at all, he thought. Horace shook his head. Even if there wasn't a dragon here, he'd still have to find one somewhere by tomorrow morning.

"Who's making all that racket on a Sunday morning?" Two golden eyes peered out at Horace from the cave.

"Um, me," said Horace. "Avaunt, dragon."

"I heard you the first time," grumbled the dragon, waddling out of the cave. "There's no need to yell."

The dragon was as high as the school roof, and its scales were a reddish gold. Horace gulped. The dragon reminded him of Dad.

But Dad's not really a dragon, Horace told himself. If Dad liked turning into an apple tree, he'd still be able to eat apple pies.

But if Dad liked being a sheep, he wondered, would he still enjoy roast lamb? Life just wasn't simple.

"Look," said the dragon. "Are you challenging me or not?"

"Yes," said Horace. He took a breath. "I'm sorry, but I have to fight you!"

"No need to apologize," said the dragon. "I'm the one with fangs and fiery breath that can cook a cow."

"Oh. I see your point," said Horace.

Something rumbled loudly. The dragon pressed its stomach. "Excuse me," it said. "I haven't had breakfast yet. Do you mind if we get on with this? Mom doesn't like it if I'm late for breakfast."

"What the heck," muttered Horace. He raised his carving knife and broomstick, and charged.

CHAPTER 14

Horace the Dragon Slayer

The dragon scratched under its wing, one eye on Horace, then bent down and grabbed Horace's broomstick.

Crunch!

The broomstick and carving knife disappeared down the dragon's throat.

The dragon burped. "Delicious," it said. "Now, are you going to try to stab me? I'll swallow you in one gulp and go eat my breakfast."

"I don't have a dagger," admitted Horace.

The dragon sighed. "Then you'd better try something else," it said.

Horace gulped. "Like what?" he asked.

"How do I know?" said the dragon. "You're the dragon slayer. I'm just a dragon."

Horace tried to think. But how could he think with a fire-breathing dragon standing over him?

What would Mom and Dad really want? A son who didn't do his homework and was expelled, or a son who'd been digested into a pile of dragon droppings?

Maybe this whole dragon hunt was a bad idea! There had to be some other way to make Sir Sneazle happy!

"Actually, Sir Dragon," began Horace.

The dragon stared. "What did you call me?" it demanded.

"Um, Sir Dragon," said Horace.

The dragon gave a howl of rage. "How dare you?" it screamed.

The fire whizzed past Horace's ear. A bush behind him burst into flames.

"What? What's wrong?" cried Horace. "I was only trying to be polite!"

"I'm a girl!" yelled the dragon.

She picked Horace up between her claws. "Can't you tell the difference between a girl dragon and a boy dragon?"

"Um," said Horace, "now that I see you closer. I mean, I've never met a dragon before, so how could I? I didn't mean to insult you!"

"Sparkie, what do you think you're doing? I've told you a thousand times not to play with your food!"

Another dragon poked a head out of the cave.

Sparkie said, "He insulted me, Mom!"

"That's no excuse for playing with him!" declared the mother dragon. "Now swallow him up. Your strawberry muffins are getting cold."

"Yes, Mom," Sparkie turned to Horace again. Her mouth opened wider.

"Stop!" Sparkie's mom cried.

Sparkie stopped. "But Mom, I'm eating him politely," she said.

The ground shook as the large dragon thundered toward them. "But it's Horace!" the mother cried. "Sparkie! Don't you recognize your cousin? It's little Horace!"

CHAPTER 15

I'm Your What?

"Cousin?" cried Horace. They were in the cave, a giant cave way down beneath the mountain. Cold drips splashed from the ceiling. It was the biggest room Horace had ever seen.

The mother dragon smiled at him, showing her long white fangs. "Now, you've met your little cousin Sparkie, haven't you?" she asked.

Horace blinked. Little Sparkie must weigh at least twenty tons, he thought. "Sort of," said Horace.

Sparkie glared at him. She still hadn't forgiven him.

"And this is your great-uncle Toaster."

"What's that?" demanded an older dragon. "Speak up!"

"This is Horace, Uncle Toaster!" roared the mother dragon. The echoes boomed around the cave, sending down a shower of dust.

"No need to yell!" Uncle Toaster held out a wrinkly claw. "Good to meet you, son!"

The mother dragon beamed. "And I'm your Aunty Fluffy!" Aunty Fluffy Dragon picked up a pile of knitting. "I love knitting," she explained.

"Um, of course," said Horace. He wanted to ask how the dragons could possibly think he was their cousin or nephew or great nephew. But how could you ask a question like that with giant creatures all smiling at you, showing their fangs and burping flames?

Being a dragon's cousin did seem like a better idea than being eaten by one.

"It's good to finally meet you!" said Aunty Fluffy with a smile. "So sad when families lose touch, isn't it? So nice you finally decided to visit us. Sparkie, eat up your muffins. You won't grow up to have a big strong flame if you don't eat your muffins. Horace, you have one too."

The smallest dragon was
looking at Horace.
"I think he's cute,"
she decided at last.
"Even if he is a human.
He can't help being dumb."

"Half human," corrected her mother,
looking at Horace. "After all, his mother
is human. You can always tell if a human
is half dragon. They have webs at the
bottoms of their fingers and their hair
shines with a touch of gold like dragon's
scales, even if it's brown or black or red.
And when they're angry, their eyes turn
red, of course."

Horace looked down at his fingers.
There were tiny webs between them.
He wondered if his hair gleamed in the
sunlight. But he couldn't be half dragon!
He couldn't! Dad just pretended to be a
dragon! Didn't he?

76

Aunty Fluffy was smiling. "Oh, Horace dear, I remember when your dad met your mom. It was so romantic! Just another case of maiden meets dragon. Your mom was collecting toad droppings in the forest for one of her spells, and your dad and I were chasing eagles. Your dad took one look at your mom and zoot!"

"Zoot?" asked Horace.

Aunty Fluffy nodded. "He stared at her and I stared at him and I knew my big brother had fallen in love!" Aunty Fluffy wiped away a tear.

"And Mom?" asked Horace.

"Oh, she screamed and ran away. You know how it is with humans. No offense," she added. "Some of my best friends used to be humans. That was in the bad old days of course, before dragons were protected."

She smiled at Horace. "Of course no dragon would ever eat a human now. Well, not often. Hardly ever. Just as a special treat sometimes if one turns up at the cave. Where was I?"

"Dad had just fallen in love with Mom," said Horace.

"Well, your dad flew after her and saw where she lived. So he started sending her presents."

"Flowers and boxes of chocolates?" asked Horace.

"Oak trees and dead eagles," said Aunty Fluffy. "He found her some toad droppings too. Your mom got mad about the mess on her doorstep every morning. Then one day she got so mad, she threatened to make a spell to send him away forever."

"Let me guess," said Horace. "It went wrong."

"How did you know?" asked Aunty Fluffy.

"Mom's spells go wrong sometimes," explained Horace.

"Well, instead of making him disappear, she accidentally turned him into a human. She fell in love with him at first sight. Well, first sight as a human. She'd seen him every day as a dragon. A few months later, they got married."

Aunty Fluffy shook her head sadly.

"Your parents decided you and your sister should be brought up only as humans. It would be too confusing for you to know your dragon relatives. But now you're here! I'm so glad they changed their minds!" Aunty Fluffy smiled again.

Horace tried to think. Dad was a dragon who changed into a human, not a human who sometimes changed into a dragon!

Mom knew! These were his relatives!

Suddenly Horace knew he had to tell the truth.

These dragons had invited him into their cave. They hadn't eaten him, even though he'd been prepared to kill one just to do his homework.

Horace knew that he'd be ashamed for the rest of his life if he didn't come clean.

Horace took a deep breath. "I haven't told you the truth!"

Aunty Fluffy stopped knitting. "You haven't?" she asked.

Horace looked down. "I didn't come here to meet my relatives. I didn't even know about you! I came here because my teacher said I had to bring a dead dragon to school for my homework!"

Aunty Fluffy blinked.

"But, Horace dear, if you had to take a dead dragon to school, why on earth didn't you ask your father?"

"Dad?"

Aunty Fluffy smiled. "Your dad could play dead better than any other dragon I've ever known. I remember once he was playing dead in the forest and this knight came along."

"You mean ask Dad to pretend to be dead?" cried Horace.

"Of course!" Aunty Fluffy raised her eyebrows. "What did you think I meant?"

CHAPTER 16

Back Home

It was fun riding home on a dragon's back. Horace stared down at the tiny cottage by the hill as Sparkie soared down and landed in the clearing.

Horace slid off her back. "Thanks!" he said. "That was great!"

Sparkie winked at him. "Any time you want to hang out or go hunting, just give me a call. I have excellent hearing." She launched herself back into the sky. Then she was above the hill and gliding home.

Horace turned and walked down the path between the guinea pig bushes.

"Is that you, Horace?" The door opened. It was Dad, in human form.

Dad looked older, decided Horace. There were shadows under his eyes that hadn't been there yesterday.

"Come inside," Dad said, opening the door wider.

Horace stepped inside without saying anything. Dad closed the front door behind him.

Horace looked around the kitchen. "Where's Mom?" he asked.

"In the cave," said Dad. "We agreed that this is a father and son thing. Mom is going to explain it to Grub."

"Would you ever have told us if I hadn't found out?" demanded Horace.

Dad shrugged. "I don't know," he admitted. "It isn't easy, telling someone a secret like that."

"But why keep it a secret?" cried Horace. "Why not just tell us?"

"Tell you what? That your dad is a dragon? I wanted you and Grub to have a normal life," said Dad. "How can you have a normal life with a dragon for a dad? What do you think your friends would say if they knew you were half dragon? Do you think the King's school would have accepted a dragon's son?"

"No," said Horace.

"I wanted you to have a human future! Is that so bad?" Dad asked.

Horace was silent for a moment. Then he whispered, "No, Dad." Dad held out his arms. Horace ran into them and Dad held him tight.

CHAPTER 17

The Plan

"So, it's settled," said Dad. It was half an hour later, and Dad was a dragon again, leaning back on the giant treasure chest he'd dragged out of the cave behind the cottage.

There was treasure in the other caves, too, Horace had discovered, as well as a giant bed and an underground lake, perfect for a dragon to swim in. There were also miles of tunnels that Horace couldn't wait to explore.

Mom sat on the other side of the table. Grub sat beside her. Grub didn't seem very excited at all to be part dragon.

Mom nodded. "I'll tell Horace's friends that I enchanted you so you look like a dead dragon." She looked guilty. "It's almost the truth, anyway," she added.

"I'll borrow a wagon," added Horace, "so we can carry Dad to school."

"I'll lie on the wagon and pretend to be dead," said Dad.

"I'm going too," said Grub, "because I'm the maiden in distress. My first day at school!"

Horace saw his friends walking up the path. Grub ran to the window. "Snidge may have knobby knees, but he has really nice eyes," she said. She did a little dance. "This is going to be so cool!"

Dad laid on the wagon with his giant wings outstretched, his tail dragging on the ground, his eyes closed, and one of his hands clutching his chest. He looked very convincing.

Bran, Snidge, Bernard, and Pol were almost speechless at the sight of him.

"I never knew dragons were so big," said Bran.

"Just look at those fangs!" murmured Snidge.

Horace smiled. It was true! Dad was the best-looking dragon he'd ever seen, even if he was pretending to be dead.

Aunty Fluffy was right. Dad was great at playing dead!

"Are you sure he'll look like a dragon all day?" asked Bran.

Horace nodded. "Mom's spell should last for hours!" he said.

The group set out.

First came Bernard, carrying the hundred pages of the History of the Sword, with no blots, thanks to Grub's invention. No spelling mistakes, either. At least Horace hoped there were no spelling mistakes.

Next came Snidge, Pol, and Bran, leading a white horse, with Grub dressed in her best clothes.

The white horse was really one of the guinea pigs. Mom had turned it into a white horse that morning.

Grub did look pretty good, thought Horace, with her long hair brushed down her back, the oil cleaned off her face, and a flowing green silk gown instead of her overalls.

Horace looked closer. Grub had tiny webs between her fingers, too, and her hair shined like dragon scales!

Next came Mom, riding Grub's new invention, the one with the two big wheels. The invention really worked well, Horace had to admit, once Mom had pulled up her skirts so they didn't get tangled in the pedals.

Horace walked behind the cart, in case Dad's tail got caught in the bushes.

High above them all, golden scales flashed in the sunlight. Sparkie? wondered Horace. Or Aunt Fluffy?

Camelot was before them now, with high city walls and thatched roofs.

And, above it all, the castle on its hill, with towers reaching to the sky.

It's a Trap!

There was no way Dad and the wagon were going to fit inside the schoolroom, so the boys lined up against the wall. Bernard went first with his report, then the three boys with Grub, and finally Horace with Dad and the wagon. Mom was hiding under some nearby trees.

"This is so exciting!" Grub said. "I'm going to meet the King!"

"Look! All the hay carts are coming this way!" Bran said.

"I wonder why they aren't going in the city gates and around to the stables," said Horace.

The hay cart drivers didn't seem to be getting off or tending to their horses, either. They just sat on their carts, leaning against the hay, like they were waiting.

Dad peered up from his wagon. "Maybe they heard that King Arthur is going to come down to the school this morning," he said. "It's not often a cart driver gets to see a king."

"But how would they know the King is coming here?" began Horace, then added, "Quick! Dad! Lie down again! Sir Sneazle is coming!"

Sir Sneazle made his way between the hay carts. Suddenly he stopped and stared, then hurried toward them. "What is going on here?"

"It's our homework, sir!" Horace said.

"Here's my report, sir," said Bernard, holding out the papers. "No blots!"

"And here's our maiden," said Bran. "We rescued her from ferocious beasts!"

"She's the fairest maiden in the country, sir," said Snidge. Grub grinned at him.

"And this," said Horace, "is my dragon!"

"You fools!" cried Sir Sneazle. "You stupid fools! I never expected any of you to actually do your homework projects! I expected you all to fail! To be too ashamed to come to school!"

Sir Sneazle waved his arms in the air. "Leg of lizard," he muttered. "Tongue of bee, let these fools stand silently!"

Suddenly Horace realized he couldn't move.

"Why do you think a knight like me is teaching in a school like this?" cried Sir Sneazle.

Suddenly trumpets sounded down the road. The King! thought Horace. King Arthur was coming!

Sir Sneazle smiled. He rubbed his hands happily. "The King!" he shouted. "That is why I took this job! To get to the King! I didn't want you brats getting in the way."

The cart drivers looked suddenly more alert. What was happening? thought Horace. What was Sir Sneazle planning?

CHAPTER 19

Dragon Anger

Sir Sneazle stood up straight and smiled as King Arthur walked toward him.

King Arthur was not alone. Behind him walked the bravest knights in the kingdom, Sir Lancelot of the Lake, Sir Galahad, Sir Kay, and Sir Gawaine.

"Welcome, your Majesty!" cried Sir Sneazle. "So good of you to visit us!"

"I'm always glad to take the time to see schoolwork," said King Arthur. "Best school in the kingdom, this one!"

Sir Sneazle waved his hands again.
"Sting of wasp and jellyfish bone, let these
knights be turned to stone!"

The King and his knights stood still.
This can't be happening! thought Horace,
trying to see everything out of the corner
of his eye.

Suddenly hay flew everywhere. Men
leaped from the hay carts, men in armor,
with swords raised.

An invasion!
thought Horace. And
none of the knights
could do anything!

Sir Sneazle laughed.
"How about we trade,
Your Majesty!" he
cried. "You can have
my school, and
I will take your
castle! King Sneazle
the First!"

He raised his arms to the troops.
"Charge!" he yelled.

No! thought Horace. It can't happen
like this! The kingdom is peaceful!

Suddenly he felt anger rise up inside
him. I've never felt anger like this before,
thought Horace.

Dragon anger!

He glanced at Grub out of the corner of his eye. It was happening to her too! We're half dragon! thought Horace. And the dragon half is taking over!

"Don't you hurt my friends!" roared Grub, unfolding her golden wings.

"You leave our kingdom alone!" yelled Horace.

Dad was rising up too, flame billowing across the ground, hot and fast. The hay was burning! The soldiers screamed, unable to run through the flames. Fire behind them, dragons in front of them.

"Unfreeze the King and his knights and my friends!" yelled Horace.

"Especially Snidge!" cried Grub. She blushed and her gold scales turned red. "He's got nice eyes," she said.

"Never!" screamed Sir Sneazle.

Hooosh! Dad rolled a carpet of flame toward him. Horace and Grub flapped their wings to push the flame along.

"Sea slug pus and spider hair, lift me up into the air!" Sir Sneazle floated above the fire.

Horace spread his wings and launched himself up.

He was flying! Up, up, up! Then he turned and swooped downward, grasping Sir Sneazle in his claws.

"Take that!" yelled Grub. She flapped up next to Horace and poked Sir Sneazle with her claws.

"I give up!" shrieked Sir Sneazle.

"Unfreeze Mom and my friends and the King and his knights!" commanded Horace.

Sir Sneazle shivered. "Seagull spit and jelly's jiggle, let all here be free to wriggle!" he yelled.

"Tell your men to put down their weapons!" ordered Horace.

"Put down your weapons!" cried Sir Sneazle as Horace gripped him. The soldiers put down their swords.

King Arthur raised his sword to Sir Sneazle. "Surrender to the might of Camelot, Sir Sneazle!" he yelled.

"I surrender!" cried Sir Sneazle.

It was over.

CHAPTER 20

A Dragon Knight

King Arthur's knights marched the Saxons off to the dungeons, with Sir Sneazle wrapped in iron chains.

No sorcerer, like Sir Sneazle, could make magic when he was touching iron. The kingdom was safe.

King Arthur gazed after the invaders, then shook his head.

"They almost succeeded," he said. "If it hadn't been for you brave dragons, they would have!"

King Arthur pointed at Horace. "Kneel down."

Horace knelt on the burned grass. The King tapped him on each shoulder with his sword. "Rise, Sir Horace, Knight and Dragon of the Round Table. You can join us when you finish your studies. You are a brave and noble knight!" he said.

The trumpets blasted, and then the King and his knights were gone.

Bran wrinkled his forehead. "I don't understand," he said. "You're not really a dragon, are you?" he asked Dad.

Dad glanced at Horace and Grub. "Yes," he said.

Bran turned to Horace and Grub. "Then you're dragons too!"

Horace lifted his chin proudly. "Half dragons!" he said.

"Cool!" yelled Bran. "Can you take us flying?"

"Well, I don't know if we can take you all flying," said Dad. "There's really only room for one person at a time on a dragon's back!"

"Don't bother about me," said Mom. She smiled at Dad. "I have a dragon of my own! I can go flying whenever I want!"

"I'll take Snidge," said Grub.

"I'll take you then," Dad said to Pol.

"I'll take Bernard," said Horace. "But what about Bran?"

"I'll take him!" someone boomed. It was Sparkie.

One by one the dragons rushed into the air. Higher and higher they flew, weaving in and out of the clouds, over the towers of Camelot, the brown fields of grain, the gold fields of hay, and the cottages. The river sparkled below them in the sunlight.

CHAPTER 21

Afterword

Camelot faded from history, and so did the dragons.

But maybe the dragons haven't really vanished. Maybe one day a kid will look at his hands and see the tiny webs between his fingers, or will look in the mirror when she's angry and see her eyes are gleaming red.

Maybe one day the dragons will throw off their human form and soar again across the skies.

About the Author

Jackie French has written more than 100 books for children and adults, many of them award winners, including her 2003 ALA Notable Book *Diary of a Wombat*. French loves wombats. In fact, she's had 39 of them! She says that one of the reasons she writes so many books is to pay the carrot bill for the furry creatures. French is a terrible speller (she's dyslexic), but a terrific writer. She lives in Australia with her husband, children, and assorted marsupials.

About the Illustrator

Stephen Michael King grew up in Sydney, Australia. When he was nine, he was partially deaf, but no one noticed that he had a hearing problem. King turned to art to communicate without using words, and eventually his illustrations won him numerous awards. He lives on an island off the coast of Australia in a mud-brick house.

⚜ Glossary ⚜

avaunt (ah-VAWNT)—a knight's way of saying "Get out!" or "Away from here!" or "Leave now!"

blot (BLAHT)—a spot or mark of ink

cauldron (CAWL-drun)—a large metal pot

convincing (kun-VINSS-ing)—looking or acting in a persuasive way

enchant (en-CHANT)—to put a spell on someone

knight (NYT)—a warrior on horseback who serves a king or queen

maiden (MAYD-uhn)—a young, unmarried woman

murmur (MUR-mur)—to speak quietly and unclearly; to complain

protected species (proh-TEK-tid SPEE-sees)—a group of creatures that it is unlawful to hunt or harm

Saxon (SAKS-un)—a group of people who invaded England in the fifth and sixth centuries

tentacle (TENT-uh-kul)—a long arm on a creature, such as an octopus or squid

⌇ Discussion Questions ⌇

1. Who do you think was the smartest person in the kingdom: Sir Sneazle, Grub, or Horace? Explain your answer.

2. Would you want to have dragons in your family? Why or why not? Would you want to be part dragon yourself?

3. Horace and his friends helped each other out with their homework. He even got his dad to pretend to be dead, and his sister to pretend that she was rescued. Do you think it was fair of them to do this? Is it a good idea to ask for help from others with homework?

ᕲᕞ Writing Prompts ᕞᕲ

1. What would you do if you could turn into a dragon at any time? Would you spend most of your time flying, or using your fiery breath? Would you help rescue people, or hunt for tasty pigs? Write about it!

2. Horace was lucky that he could still turn into a dragon after Sir Sneazle put a spell on him. What would have happened if Horace and Grub had not turned into dragons? What else could they have done to defeat the invading Saxons? Write down your solution.

⌣ Internet Sites ⌣

Do you want to know more about subjects related to this book? Or are you interested in learning about other topics? Then check out FactHound, a fun, easy way to find Internet sites.

Our investigative staff has already sniffed out great sites for you!

Here's how to use FactHound:

1. Visit *www.facthound.com*

2. Select your grade level.

3. To learn more about subjects related to this book, type in the book's ISBN number: **1598893432**.

4. Click the **Fetch It** button.

FactHound will fetch the best Internet sites for you!